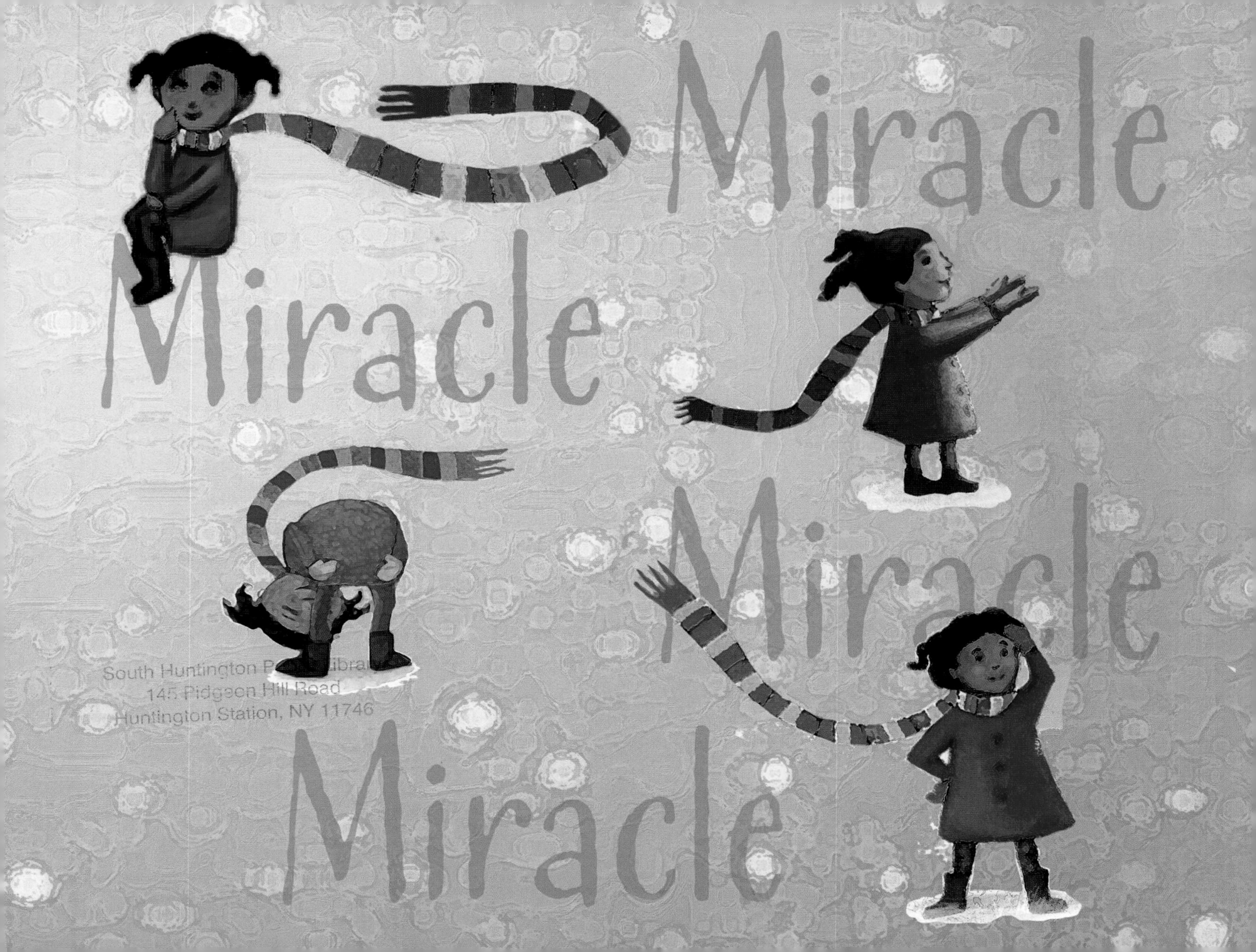
Miracle
Miracle
Miracle
Miracle

For Khairi, Khyla and Marquetta may your lives be filled with miracles both large and small.
–Love C.A.H

To Uncle Bob for one miraculous winter day. And with love to my curious explorers, Alek and Max.
–L.A.H

For information contact Chanavia Haddock at chaddock@chanavia.com.

Written by Chanavia Haddock · Illustrated by Liz Amini-Holmes · Designed by Liz Amini-Holmes
·Edited by · Chanavia Haddock · Creative Direction by Chanavia Haddock

Library of Congress Registration Number: TXu 1-932-700

ISBN: 978-1-48358-660-1

Introducing
Piper Rose

Miracle, miracle

where are you?

I've searched...

MIRA

and searched...

...the whole day through.

I've searched up high.

ACLE

I've searched down low.

I've even looked beneath

the snow.

Miracle, miracle

there you are!

In the sky...

among the stars.

The End

29 99